The M.C. Gang

by Jean L

illustrated by Al

CW01021456

Contents

The M.C. Gang

Hi! We're the M.C. Gang. We all live in the Pinetree Flats, in Marston Court, London.

Hi! I'm Omar, and I'm nine years old. I love football, TV and alligators. I'm the eldest so naturally I'm the leader of the M.C. Gang.

Hi! My name's Lily, and I'm nearly nine. I adore ice-skating, pizza and puppies. Omar thinks he's leader, but actually I am.

Hi! I'm Tim and I'm eight. I won't be nine for ages. I'm keen on football, computers, chips and killer sharks.

Hi! My name's Rosie and I'm six. I'm Lily's sister. I love ballet, pizza and puppies. I think the M.C. Gang is really cool!

Marston Court

The M.C. Gang Investigates in ...
Tim the Detective

Lily was on the phone to Omar.

"Come over! Quick!" she cried. "Bring Tim! We've got something to show you."

Omar and Tim rushed round to Lily's flat. She and Rosie were waiting for them.

"Look!" Rosie pointed to a basket in the corner.

"A puppy!" exclaimed Tim.

"Isn't she cute?" said Lily. "Mum collected her from the animal shelter. She'd been abandoned."

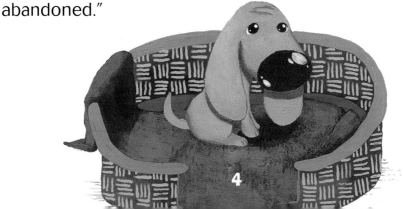

The puppy's name was Taz. She jumped out of her basket on wobbly legs. Tim laughed. Taz was wagging her tail so hard that her bottom wagged with it.

"Hey, she licked me!" cried Omar.

"That's what dogs do," said Lily smugly. "Hold out your hand and she'll do it again."

So Omar held out his hand and Taz licked it again. Her whiskers tickled and Omar giggled. The puppy became excited. She leapt onto a chair and snatched an envelope off the table.

5

Taz ran all round the kitchen,
with the envelope in her mouth.

"Quick, get it off her!" hissed Lily.
"Before Mum comes in."

The M.C. Gang charged after
the puppy.

Tim grabbed hold of the
envelope and tugged.
The puppy tugged back.
"Watch out, you'll tear it!"
cried Lily.

Too late! The envelope was
ripped into three pieces.

"Oh!" cried Tim, as a £2 coin fell out.

Omar snatched the coin. Lily grabbed
the bits of envelope.

"Look at that!" said Lily, crossly. "It was a letter. Now you've gone and torn it!"

"Sorry," mumbled Tim.

The letter was now torn into three. One piece looked like this:

Another looked like this:

And the third looked like this:

"How can anyone read it now?" wailed Lily.

Tim hung his head. Omar began trying to fit the pieces together like a jigsaw.

First he tried:

Then he tried:

END OF THE ROAD ANIMAL SHELTER
POSY AND BEN
SAY "PLEASE HELP US!"

Dear Friend,
If you would like to help animals like Posy and Ben, please fill in your name and address below. Thank you.
Best wishes
Susan Smith
Manager

NAME: Mrs Jackson
ADDRESS: Flat 16, Pinetree Flats, Marston Court, London

"Oh! It's the shelter," said Lily, "where Taz came from."

Rosie ran to fetch some sticky tape and they stuck the letter back together. Lily put it on the table with the £2 coin.

"Mum," she called, "Taz tore your letter!"

Mum didn't seem too annoyed. "Puppies will be puppies," she said. "Now, then. Your tea's ready. I've put it in the other room. We'll shut Taz out here."

"Oh, Mum! No!" begged Rosie.

"Sorry," said her mum firmly. "She's not yet house-trained. I don't want a mess on my new carpet! It's time she quietened down, anyway."

Mum returned Taz to her basket and warned her sternly to be a good girl. Then they all went into the other room to have tea.

"I'm just popping down to the shops," said Mum. "I won't be long. Be good! Leave Taz in the kitchen. All right?"

When Mum had gone, poor Taz started to cry. She was lonely in the kitchen.

Rosie couldn't bear it. "I'm going to give her a cuddle!" she said. Lily decided to join her.

"She's still crying," said Rosie, as she and Lily emerged from the kitchen.

"I'll go and cheer her up," said Tim.

Tim and Taz had a great game with a ball of silver paper. The puppy chased it all round the kitchen, then took it back to her bed to bury it.

She lifted up a corner of her blanket with her teeth and carefully hid the silver paper under it. Then she pushed the blanket flat again with her nose. After that, she trampled round for a bit, gave a big sigh and lay down.

"She seems to be tired, now," said Tim, as he rejoined the others.

The children finished their tea, and Lily turned on the TV.
The girls' mum returned from the shops.

"Excellent," she said. "Taz is fast asleep."

"That's because I played with her," said Tim.

As Tim spoke, there was a knock at the door.
Taz immediately woke up
and started barking.

WOOF!

WOOF!

"That will be Miss Stewart," said Mum. "She's come to
collect some money for the animal shelter. I'll just go and
give it to her."

A few seconds later, Mum put her head round the door and said, "Has anyone seen the £2 coin I left out for Miss Stewart?"

"Yes, it was on the kitchen table," said Lily.

"It seems to have vanished," said Mum.

They all went into the kitchen to look for it. Tim could remember seeing it on the table. But it wasn't there now.

"Oh, well. Never mind. I expect it will turn up," said Mum.

She didn't ask any of the M.C. Gang if they had taken it. She trusted Lily and Rosie because they were her children. She trusted Omar because Omar's mum was a special friend of hers. But did she trust Tim?

Tim worried about it all evening. Everyone knew his dad was out of work and that his family was short of money. What if the girls' mum thought that Tim had stolen the £2?

When Tim got home, his mum noticed that he was unhappy.

"What's wrong?" she asked. "You're very quiet."

"Lily's mum lost some money," mumbled Tim.

"Really? How did that happen?"

"It was on the kitchen table, then she couldn't find it.

She might think it was me!"

Tim's mum looked at him.

"Was it you?"

"No!" said Tim.

"Then you have nothing to worry about."

But Tim couldn't stop himself. He worried and worried.

In the end, Tim sat down at his mum's PC and made out a list.

SUSSPECKS

"That's not the correct spelling," said his mum. "It's like this." She leaned over and typed it out: *SUSPECTS*.

"Go away!" grumbled Tim. This was private. He objected to his mum looking over his shoulder.

SUSPECTS

Suspect 1: Rosie. She went into the kitchen to cuddle Taz.

Suspect 2: Lily. She also went into the kitchen to cuddle Taz.

Suspect 3: Tim. He went into the kitchen and played with Taz.

Suspect 4:

He stopped. Suspect 4 was Omar. But had Omar gone into the kitchen? Yes! He had!

Suspect 4: Omar. He went into the kitchen to get some milk.

They had all gone into the kitchen! Any of them could have taken the money. But Tim knew that he hadn't, and he felt sure that none of the others had. They weren't thieves.

Suddenly he had an idea.

It made no sense, though.

Suspect 5: Lily's mum. She went into the kitchen.

Why would Lily's mum steal her own money?

Then another idea occurred to him ...

15

Could somebody have climbed in through the window?

The flat was on the ground floor, but the window had been closed. And anyway, Taz would have barked. Hmm, thought Tim. He would have to do a lot of thinking ...

Next day, the M.C. Gang met up again. "Did your mum find her money?" enquired Omar.

"No, we've hunted all over," replied Lily.

"Mum thinks we took it!" wailed Rosie.

"She doesn't," retorted Lily. "We told her we didn't, and she believes us."

"So what can have happened to it?" said Omar.
There was a silence. Tim cleared his throat.

"I've been thinking," he said. "I've got an idea ..."

They all returned to the girls' flat.

"Tim wants to show us something," said Lily to her mum.

"It's just an idea," muttered Tim. He was starting to feel
a bit foolish. But he had ruled out Omar, he had ruled
out Lily and Rosie, he had ruled out their mum; and it
certainly wasn't him! So who else was there?

Everyone followed Tim into the kitchen. Tim knelt by the
side of Taz's basket. Taz thought it was another game!
Slowly, holding his breath, Tim lifted up the corner of
Taz's blanket ...

Phew! Tim let out his breath in a big whoosh. There, under the blanket, was the ball of silver paper which Taz had buried. And there, next to the silver paper, was – a £2 coin!

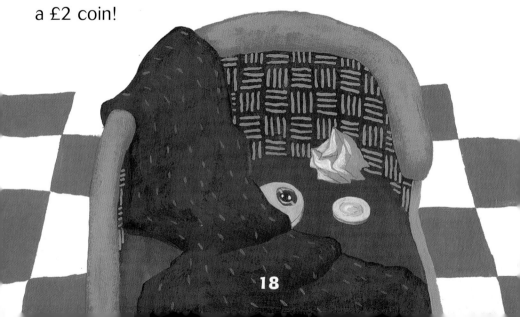

"Yes!" Rosie clapped her hands. "Clever Tim!"
The girls' mum burst out laughing. "That naughty puppy!
She must have jumped onto a chair and taken it."

"And look what else is there!" cried Lily.
"Look, Mum, it's your brooch! You've
been looking everywhere for that."

"Well done!" Omar thumped Tim
on the back. "You deserve a medal!"

"If you ask me," said the girls' mum,
"he deserves a reward. What shall we give him?"

"Give him the £2!" answered Rosie.

The M.C. Gang Investigates in ...
The Case of the Flower Thief

Omar, Lily, Tim and Rosie were sitting on the grass
outside the old people's block. They weren't making any
noise. They were just sitting there quietly, minding their
own business, when old Mr Bradley came hobbling out.

"Hey! You lot!" he shouted.

"Us?" said Lily.

"Yes! You! I want a word with you."

"We're not doing anything," said Omar.

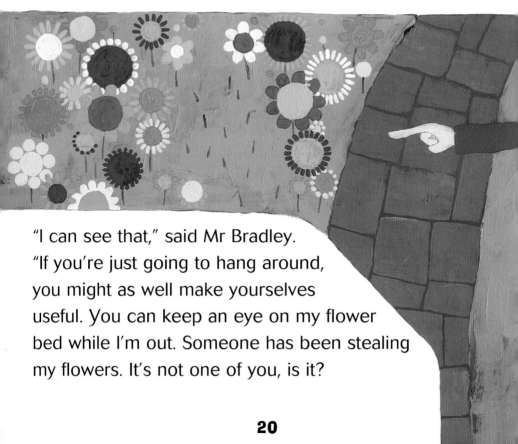

"I can see that," said Mr Bradley.
"If you're just going to hang around,
you might as well make yourselves
useful. You can keep an eye on my flower
bed while I'm out. Someone has been stealing
my flowers. It's not one of you, is it?

"No, it is not!" responded Lily.

"It must be someone that comes visiting," said Mr Bradley. "They might still be in there. So just keep your eyes open. All right?"

"How long for?" asked Omar.

"I'll be gone for a couple of hours," replied Mr Bradley.

"A couple of hours?" cried Rosie. She was only six, and a couple of hours seemed like a really long time. It did to the others, too.

"I'm not sure." Tim shook his head. "Suppose I get hungry?"

"You catch that thief," said Mr Bradley, "and I'll give you ... a pound!"

"Pound each?" said Omar.

"Pound between you."

"No way!" said Omar.

Mr Bradley grumbled, but in the end he agreed that if the Gang caught the thief, he would give them 50p ... each.

"Done! It's a deal!" smiled Omar.

For two whole hours, the Gang sat on the grass and watched the old people's block.

"I'm getting bored," moaned Rosie.

"I'm getting hungry," said Tim.

"We can't leave," insisted Lily. "We're being paid. We're private detectives!"

Not many people came or went. The postman arrived and said, "Good morning!" He wasn't a very likely thief.

The old lady from flat number one came out with her shopping trolley and smiled at them. She wasn't a very likely thief either.

Then a boy came out. He was about twelve years old, with bright red hair.

Lily poked Tim in the ribs and hissed, "Ask him!"

"Ask him what?" said Tim.

"If he likes flowers!" said Lily.

But Tim wasn't keen, and nor was Omar. This boy looked like the sort who might beat up people.

"Useless!" said Mr Bradley, when he came back and heard the Gang's report. "Didn't you even find out who the boy was visiting?"

Omar said that it either had to be the old lady in flat number three or the old lady in flat number two. "One or the other."

"Fat lot of help that is!" said Mr Bradley. "Just look at my flower bed!"

They did look. There was a row of holes where someone had pulled up Mr Bradley's plants.

"That didn't happen while we were here," said Omar.

"No," said Mr Bradley. "It was earlier. The thief has obviously been indoors all this time. And you let him escape! Well, that's it. You didn't catch him, so you don't get paid. If you want to earn your money you'd better come back again tomorrow. Early, mind! I'm going out at nine o'clock. You'll have to be here by then."

The children walked slowly back to their own block.

"It's not fair!" cried Rosie. "We sat there for hours!"

"Yes, and we might sit there for hours tomorrow," said Omar. "And still not get paid."

Lily said that they should write out an agreement and get Mr Bradley to sign it.

"We'll go to your place," she said to Tim, "and do it there."

This was the Gang's agreement:

Flat 4
Pinetree Flats
Marston Court
15th August

Dear M.C. Gang,

I agree to pay you 50p each if you keep watch over my flowers.

_____

Mr Bradley

PS 50p is for two hours of watching. After two hours it will cost an extra 50p per hour.

Next morning, just before nine a.m., the M.C. Gang knocked at Mr Bradley's door.

"This letter is the agreement," said Omar. "You need to sign it on the line above your name."

Mr Bradley said, "I don't know what kids are coming to!" But he signed the letter.

"You just keep an eye on those flowers," he said. "I don't want to come back and find any more gone."

They took it in turns to watch the flowers. Rosie and Lily did the first hour, then Omar, then Tim. Lily and Omar both said they didn't see anybody – not even the postman. Tim didn't see anybody either, but that was because he fell asleep. He woke with a start, almost an hour later.

Help! Help!

Another clump of flowers had gone!

The thief had been there and Tim hadn't spotted him! He stared up at the flats – and there, at the window of flat number three, was the boy with red hair. He *had* to be the thief!

The boy came out while Tim was still wondering what to do. He scowled at Tim who then broke into goose pimples. He broke into even more goose pimples when the rest of the Gang returned and he had to confess that he had fallen asleep.

"But I know who it is! I know who's doing it. It's that boy!" said Tim.

"The one with the red hair?" said Lily. "It can't be!"

"But he was here," said Tim. "I saw him!"

"So did we," said Rosie. "We saw him out shopping!"

Lily said that she and Rosie had gone out with their mum and had seen the red-haired boy in the supermarket with his mum. "So he couldn't be the thief!"

"You're just making it up," said Omar, "aren't you?"

"I'm not!" said Tim. But nobody believed him.

Mr Bradley swore quite badly when he discovered that more of his flowers had gone. He paid the Gang, but even Lily and Omar felt bad about taking it.

Tim felt worse than anyone. He worried about it all day long. He knew he had seen the boy but how could he prove it? And how could the boy have been in two places at once? There was only one way to find out.

After his tea, Tim plucked up the courage to go back to the old people's block. He rang the bell at flat number three.

An old lady opened the door. She was hobbling with a walking stick. "I have bad knees," she said. "But I'm so fortunate! My grandson visits me every day. He brought me these beautiful flowers ... look! Aren't they lovely?"

Tim looked, and gulped. How could he tell the old lady that the flowers came from Mr Bradley's flower bed?

"These are my grandsons," said the old lady. She pointed to a photo. "But only Donny visits me."

Tim's jaw fell open. "W-which one is Donny?" he asked.

"Donny's the one on the left," said the old lady.

Ten minutes later, Omar was surprised to get an e-mail:

Dear Gang

I have sloved the mistri! They are IDENTIKLE TWOBS.

Tim

Omar took the e-mail downstairs to the ground floor, where Lily and Rosie lived.

"Look," he said. "I've had an e-mail from Tim. Do you think it's in code?"

Lily studied it a while. "No," she said. "It's just Tim's spelling. Plus he's hit the wrong keys!"

"So what does it say?" demanded Rosie.

"I have solved the mystery," said Lily. "They are identical twins ..."

Next morning, the children met up as usual.

"What shall we do today?" asked Lily.

Tim said that they must go and keep watch again.

"*Again*?" said Lily.

Tim said, "Yes, and this time, we'll catch him in the act!"

"It could be dangerous," said Omar. "And Mr Bradley won't even pay us!"

Tim said that they would just have to do it for nothing. They owed it to Mr Bradley.

"I don't like Mr Bradley," said Rosie. "And anyway, I'm bored with this game!"

"Well, I'm going," said Tim, "even if I have to go by myself."

There was a silence. Then, sighing, Omar said, "I suppose we'd better come with you in case he tries bashing you."

Poor Donny! He wasn't a bashing kind of boy at all. He was big, and he looked tough, but he was quite frightened when the Gang jumped out and accused him of stealing flowers.

"I didn't know they were proper planted ones," he said. "I thought they were just growing there, by themselves. I just wanted to make my nan happy!"

He said that his nan loved flowers, but could never afford to buy them.

Just then Mr Bradley came out. "What she needs," he said, "is a window box. You and me, my boy, will make her one. Oh, and you lot!" He turned to the Gang. "You're not quite as useless as I thought. Here! Have some loose change."

He emptied out his pocket and pressed a pile of coins into Rosie's hand. "Don't spend it all at once!"

Mr Bradley and Donny went off to make their window box. The Gang wandered happily off towards the shops with the pile of money.

"Just think," said Lily a bit later, through a mouthful of crisps, "it was Tim who *sloved the mistri*!"

The M.C. Gang Investigates in ...
The Great Play Petition

It was half term, and the M.C. Gang was bored. There was nothing to do, and there was nowhere to go. There wasn't even anywhere to play. In front of the Gang's block of flats there was a patch of grass with a big notice. It said:

No Games.

The grown-ups had put the notice there. They didn't want children clumping about on their grass.

At the back of the block, in front of the old people's flats, there was another patch of grass, with another notice. This one said: **Keep Off**.

The old people didn't even want children *walking* on their grass.

Lily and Rosie tried doing handstands against the back wall, but Rosie fell down and hurt herself. Grass would have been soft, but concrete was hard.

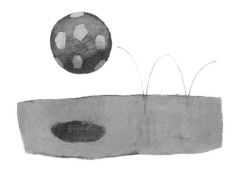

Tim and Omar kicked their football. They did their best to keep it on the path, but the path was too narrow. The ball went bouncing off across the grass.

As Omar ran after it, old Mr Bradley rushed out and started shouting, "See that notice? See what it says? Keep off the grass!"

Omar scooped up his football and ran back to join the others.

"It's so unfair!" said Lily. "We can't play anywhere."

Later on, while Lily was eating her tea, she grumbled to her mum and dad about it.

"We're not allowed to play anywhere!"

Lily's mum and dad were not really listening. They were busy talking. They wanted speed humps in the road outside the flats.

"We've organised a petition," said Lily's mum, "and we've got people to sign it."

"What's a petition?" asked Lily.

"This." Lily's mum picked up a pile of paper and showed it to Lily. The petition said:

The residents of Marston Court would like the council to put speed humps in Marston Way.

Name	Address	Signature
Alan Davis	17 Pinetree Flats, Marston Court	A. Davis
Mrs Edwards	18 Pinetree Flats, Marston Court	H. E. Edwards

"We've got lots of signatures," said Mum. "Now we'll send it to the council with this letter. When they see how many people have signed – well! We hope they'll take some notice."

The letter read:

16 Pinetree Flats
Marston Court
Marston Way
London
29th May

Dear Sir or Madam

The residents of Marston Court are worried about the speed of traffic in Marston Way.

We have signed a petition to ask the council to put speed humps in the road. We hope you will think about our idea.

Yours faithfully

Anna Jackson

Anna Jackson

"What if they don't take any notice?" asked Lily.

"Then we'll have to try something else," said Dad. "Get a story in the local paper, maybe. But first of all, we'll try the petition. That's the best way to start."

"That's the best way to start," said Lily, as the Gang met up next morning. "A petition. Like this ... look!" She showed them the one her mum had done. "See? Only ours won't be for speed humps, of course."

"What will ours be for?" asked Rosie.

"Ours will be for somewhere to play. It'll be a play petition," said Lily. "Let's decide what to put." Omar suggested:

Let children play games
and sit on the grass
and do handstands and
turn cartwheels
whenever they want.

Lily said that was too long. She said, "It's got to be something simple, like ..."

We think kids
should have somewhere
to play.

So that was what they decided. Tim said that he would print it all out nicely, using his mum's computer.

"Let's meet again after lunch," said Omar.

"Yes, and bring the petition!" added Lily.

They all met up again at two o'clock. Tim had the petition with him. Lily's jaw fell open as she read it. It said:

PLAY PETITION

We think kids should have somewhere to play and have chips for dinner.

Name	Signature
Name	Signature

"What have chips got to do with it?" asked Omar.

Tim said that he liked chips. He said there hadn't been any in the school canteen for ages and he'd just thought, if they were getting up a petition, it would be a good idea to put the chips in as well.

"But we're not talking about chips!" cried Lily, and she angrily crossed it out with a pen.

"Now you've gone and mucked it up!" said Tim.

"It can't be helped," said Lily "We can't mess around doing another one.

We've got to get started!"

By teatime, they had collected twenty-six signatures.

"Another three and we'll have a full page!" smiled Lily. "Let's try the old people."

There were ten flats in the old people's block. Surely they would be able to get three more signatures?

Two old ladies who lived on the first floor signed.

"I quite agree with you!" said one. "You *should* have somewhere to play."

"What a good idea!" said the other. "Of course I'll sign."

Omar rubbed his hands. "Nearly there!"

Nearly there – but not quite.

Mr Bradley, who had shouted at them said, "I'm not signing your petition!" and he slammed the door.

The old lady who lived in the flat opposite thought the Gang had found her missing cat. She was very upset when she discovered they just wanted her to sign a petition.

She put her glasses on to read it and said, "Oh, dear. No! I'm sorry. I'm afraid I can't possibly sign this. Chips are so bad for you!"

"The chips bit is crossed out," said Lily. But the old lady didn't seem to hear her.

"Please keep a lookout for my cat," she said. "Her name's Kitty. She's all white, with a black spot. I do so want her back!"

Lily and Omar were very cross. They were cross with the old lady for not listening, and cross with Tim for putting chips into the petition.

"If it hadn't been for you, she would have signed!" said Lily

Tim felt sorry for the old lady. "I think we ought to go and look for her cat," he said.

"So do I," said Rosie. "Poor Kitty!"

Lily and Omar huffed a bit, but in the end they agreed.

"We can't play football," said Omar, "so I suppose we might as well."

"Yes, and you never know," said Lily. "If we find her cat, she might sign our petition!"

After their tea, the Gang set off round the block. They peered into gardens and underneath cars, calling, "Kitty, Kitty, Kitty!"

After a bit, Lily and Omar wanted to give up, but Tim said, "Not yet! We haven't looked round by the garages."

There was a whole row of garages, behind the old people's block. The very last garage was empty. That was because it was haunted. Everybody knew it was haunted. But it was the only place they hadn't looked ...

"I'm not going in there!" said Lily.

Omar wasn't, either. But Tim crept up, slowly, on tiptoe. "Kitty!" he called. "Are you there?"

"Tim, come back!" begged Rosie.

Tim could hear a strange, thin, wailing, coming from inside the garage.

Meep! Meep! Meep!

He was very frightened. It was only the thought of the old lady that made him brave. He took a deep breath and squeezed in through the half-open door.

Something brushed against his cheek. **Ugh!**

A spider's web! Tim shuddered. He hated spiders!

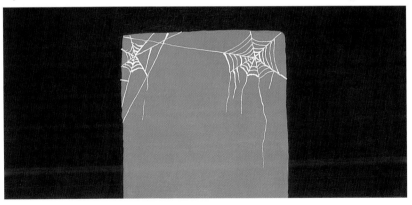

His heart began to hammer. He almost went rushing back out. But he remembered the old lady – *"Please keep a look out for my cat! I do so want her back."* – and he just stayed put.

"Kitty, Kitty, Kitty?" he whispered.

It was really dark inside
the garage. Strange shapes
loomed. Something caught in
Tim's hair.

Tim screeched, "**Aaah!**
What was that?" It was just
a piece of rope!

He'd had enough of this! He
turned to run – and
then, through the gloom, he caught a glimpse of
something white.

Meep!

"K-K-Kitty?" he said.

"Meep!" cried Kitty.

Poor Kitty! She was all caught up in a tangle of wires.
Without Tim, she might never have been freed.

The old lady wept tears of joy when she saw Kitty.
"Oh, you are such good children!" she said.

Lily couldn't help wishing they had brought the petition with them. Omar said that tomorrow they would come back and ask the old lady if she would sign it.

"She should do," he said. "Now we've found her cat for her."

But when they went back the next day, the old lady said there wasn't any need for the petition.

"You can play here, on the grass," she said. "I've spoken to the others, and they've all agreed."

"Even ... Mr Bradley?" said Omar, pointing at the old man's door.

"Poor Mr Bradley!" said the old lady. "He's not nearly such a crosspatch as he makes out. He won't mind you playing, just so long as you do it quietly."

"We'll be as quiet as mice," promised Lily.

"But do remember," said the old lady. "Not too many chips!"

"Too many chips?" said Tim. "How can you possibly have too many chips?"